The Fantastical Flying

FELIX

In Central Park

Karen Furst and James Ainsworth

AuthorHouse™
1663 Liberty Drive
Bloomington, IN 47403
www.authorhouse.com
Phone: 1 (800) 839-8640

This book is printed on acid-free paper.

ISBN: 978-1-7283-4096-8 (sc)
ISBN: 978-1-7283-4098-2 (hc)
ISBN: 978-1-7283-4097-5 (e)

Library of Congress Control Number: 2019921249

Print information available on the last page.

Published by AuthorHouse 06/17/2020

authorHOUSE®

FELIX

TAKES LINC & BILLY ON A SUPER ADVENTURE THROUGH CENTRAL PARK

Snow was rapidly inching up the sides of Billy's boots as he waited outside school for Linc. He stomped his feet to keep them warm but Billy really didn't mind the cold or the waiting. He knew that at any moment Linc would burst through the door and their day would truly begin.

Billy knew that he and Linc were lucky. Not only were they best friends, but they were a team and relied on each other. Linc was brave and daring. Billy was thoughtful and cautious. Billy appreciated that when you have a friend who is fearless, every day held the possibility of experiencing a great adventure. Just as Linc counted on Billy's nature to keep them safe!

The two boys had been best friends forever. They had lived in the same towering brick apartment building in New York City since they were toddlers. Their building sat at the edge of an enormous green wonderland called Central Park. Now that they were old enough, Linc and Billy played in the park after school and on weekends whenever they could. They liked to pretend that it was their own gigantic backyard. Not far inside the park was a special place that no one else knew about. It was their secret.

Although it was late March, the snow continued to come down fast and heavy. The boys realized that this storm would most likely be the last of the season. It was a perfect afternoon to go sledding in the park, but neither Linc nor Billy owned a sled.

As they passed by the park entrance, they viewed the other kids sliding down the hill.

Billy sighed, "I wish we had a sled."

Linc suggested that there might there be an old sled in the basement of their apartment house. So they decided to find out.

The sign to the basement entry read,

Do Not Enter!

"I'm really scared," said Billy. "We shouldn't do this, what happens if we are caught?"

Linc was absolutely certain that they would find a sled and no one would ever find out. Billy hesitantly gave in.

The metal basement door was heavy and squeaked loudly as they tugged and pulled on the handle. It took the both of them to move it. So, working together they dragged open the door and peered down into the dark and creepy basement.

The only light came from the giant furnace. It glowed yellow and orange into the darkness. Cautiously, they made their way down the steps to the lower floor. The boys peered into the gloom. Boxes, crates and barrels were piled high in one corner with old chairs and tables.

"I bet we can find a sled over there," encouraged Linc. "Let's go!"

After tossing their coats and backpacks onto the floor, they began to pull down boxes, then barrels, then chairs and tables and stacked them near the furnace. Still, no sled.

Neither boy wanted to give up easily, so they just kept digging farther into the jumble of rubbish. The pile by the furnace grew higher and higher when at last they spotted a rusty old Flexible Flyer. Thrilled with their find, they wiped it off with their shirttails. It was a great sled! Now they could fly down the hills in the park.

But what should they do with all of the boxes, crates, barrels, chairs and tables? They realized they had no choice but to restack everything! They knew it would take forever. Soon it would be dark outside, too late to go sledding.

Reluctantly, they decided to put the sled aside. They really needed to clean up this mess before they were found out by the super of the building. All of the residents knew that he checked the furnace each night without fail. So they started the difficult task. They worked and worked and stacked and stacked.

It seemed like hours later and there was just one lonely crate left sitting by the hot burning furnace.

$\mathcal{B}$illy started to pick it up when he noticed that the straw filling was moving. Something was alive inside the box!

"Linc, come here!"

"What's going on?"

Without hesitation, Linc swiftly reached down and pulled away the old straw. Under the layer of straw was a large eggshell with many cracks and openings. It was rocking back and forth. Peering out was a tiny face. It was just opening its eyes. A strange creature was squirming out of the shell!

Out popped a light green head with round hooded eyes. This head was crowned with a dark green fringe. It struggled to break the shell as it wriggled out more and more! Soon a scaly body with squat legs appeared. Finally, a long tail with a spiny end emerged with a flip!

Billy and Linc were speechless. They just stared and stared without making a sound. Was this real? How could it be? Were they really seeing a strange lizard hatch in their apartment basement?

This amazing lizard's face turned up, opened its eyes wide and smiled at them. The biggest happy smile. Then it blinked its eyes and smiled at them even wider!

Linc and Billy bent down together and knelt on the hard stone floor. Linc daringly reached into the crate and touched the scaly creature. It moved closer and closer to him.

"I think it wants us to hold it," said Linc.

"I don't know," said Billy, "What if it bites?"

Linc ignored him as he picked up the colorful lizard. It cuddled against him just like a little puppy.

"I think we discovered a new pet," said Linc.

"Shouldn't we tell someone?" asked Billy.

"NO, if we tell anyone they will just take him away from us. You know that no pets are allowed in the building. We will just hide him and take care of him. He will be our secret. You can't tell anyone! You have to promise," insisted Linc.

"Ok, I promise, but we need to feed him if we keep him," reasoned Billy. "How do we do that?"

"I know," said Linc, "go get a bottle of your sister's milk, all babies need milk."

Swiftly, Billy ran up the basement steps and scooted down the long hallway to the elevators. He pushed number ten for his floor. Luckily, he had his own key to the apartment. He peeked in. Mom and Baby Katie were in her room listening to music and didn't hear him. Tiptoeing to the kitchen, he snatched a bottle out of the refrigerator and he was down to the basement in a flash.

He found Linc rocking back and forth with the lizard tucked in his arms.

"Great, let's see if he drinks the bottle," Linc urged.

The reptile baby sucked on the bottle just like all babies do. It seemed calm and happy.

"Now we need to name him," said Linc.

"What should we call him?" replied Billy.

Suddenly, the lizard raised his tail and flapped it up and down.

"Let's call him Flipper," said Billy.

"No, we should give him a proper name like Fred or James or Pete," reasoned Linc. "Hey, how about Felix, after the super, since we found him in the furnace room?"

"I like that," said Billy. "Now we have our very own lizard with a "super" name."

FELIX!

It wasn't long before the boys realized that they had a really enormous problem. They wanted to keep Felix, but where could they hide him? The basement? NO, the super would see him. Their rooms? NO, their mothers might find him. The apartment storage lockers? NO, too many people go in and out. Their secret hideout in the park? YES! It was perfect!

Next problem. How to get him to the park without being seen? Sneaking out of their building carrying a baby reptile in a crate would not be easy! So they made a plan.

After carefully covering the box with straw, Linc lifted it up into his arms. Billy grabbed their two knapsacks. Then, remembering to act as if nothing was unusual, they walked right out the front door, waved to the doorman and headed to the park. It was almost dark and the park lights were coming on as they hurried to their secret place.

Not too far into the park, tucked under an old stone stairway, was a small abandoned storage room. They had discovered it last summer and made it their own, never telling anyone what they had found.

The moldy old metal door groaned open to reveal a snug hideaway. All last summer they had fixed it up with discards they had collected. A sleeping bag lined the floor. In the corner was an old wooden box topped with a camp lantern. They even had an old red wagon. Best of all, the room remained warm from steam pipes that crossed the ceiling. They knew that Felix would be safe and warm away from prying eyes.

Winter turned quickly to spring and the snow melted and the trees and flowers began to blossom in the park. Billy and Linc made sure to care for Felix after school and on weekends. Still, no one suspected their secret.

To their amazement, Felix grew very quickly and started to sprout little wings. He was growing more and more each day. His scales were changing into various shades of green and yellow. Before long he could barely turn around in their hiding place.

Billy and Linc felt a great responsibility for Felix. They needed to keep him safe from harm. The boys knew that despite his appearance, Felix was very gentle and loving. But would other people believe his tender nature? How long could they protect him from detection? In fear that he might be taken from them, they decided to spend as much time as they could with him before their secret was discovered.

It was on one warm spring night that the boys opened the storage room door to find Felix completely transformed! He was enormous and bumping his wings into the sidewalls of his shelter. They no longer had a lizard but a full-grown dragon as a pet!

How could they explain this? No one would believe it. They could hardly believe it. Could they possibly keep him? All of these questions spun in their heads.

As summer approached, the boys would sneak Felix out at dusk when the park was quiet. He loved to be outside and spread his wings away from the cramped hideout. On one such night, to their astonishment, Felix raised his large wings, flapped them and slowly rose off the ground! Billy and Linc fell back on the grass in shock as Felix flew in low circles over their heads. He loved it!

Now they found that they could hardly wait for dark. It meant nights of wonder. Felix swooped down under the bridges and did great loops over the trees. Always returning to get hugs from the boys.

Felix had grown large enough for the boys to ride on his back, but they knew that they could very easily fall off when he soared over the treetops.

"I would love to fly with Felix," sighed Billy.

"Maybe we can," suggested Linc.

"How?" asked Billy.

"I have been dreaming about that too and I think I have a plan," replied Linc.

It seemed as if Linc always had a plan, thought Billy, and he was certain that it involved a risky adventure as usual. But even timid Billy was so excited at the possibility of flying that he was willing to forget caution.

Not far from their hideout was the old Claremont Riding Academy. It had closed a few years ago. With luck, they might find some equipment that was left behind. Linc decided that they should head there to explore.

Crawling through a broken window was easy. The hard part was finding something that would work.

Surprisingly, lots of equipment was left behind when the stable was abandoned. Sure enough, Linc found a child's size saddle. It was just what they needed! It was made of smooth leather with straps that they could wrap around Felix.

"We need reins to hang on or we will still fall off," worried Billy.

"No problem, we can make some from the extra straps," assured Linc.

Their wagons filled with everything they needed to take a test flight. As they slowly pulled it to the secret place, Billy became more and more worried. What if they fell? Would Felix be able to carry their weight? What would happen if someone saw them?

Trying very hard not to show his fear, he trudged along, dragging his feet. Meanwhile, Linc was whistling a happy tune, excited by the prospect of another great adventure.

Later that week the boys carefully fitted the saddle on Felix. As expected, Linc was first to mount and grasp the reins. Billy was still very fearful but he trusted Linc while Felix smiled with encouragement. So Billy held his breath, climbed on and wrapped his arms around Linc's waist. Before he knew it, Felix soared into the night sky.

This was to be the first of many spectacular night rides flying high over New York City. Billy and Linc found that everything looked different from above. Their view of their city was expanding with each adventure.

Billy found that he was overcoming his fear and welcoming the prospects of new experiences. Linc learned to respect the care and caution that Felix took to see that they were secure on his back.

*B*illy and Linc treasured these summer adventures spent with Felix. One night, they might zoom by towering buildings, and the next, circle the Statue of Liberty's crown. At other times Felix would swoop down over the boats in the harbor and then head north to the George Washington Bridge. It seemed that each flight was filled with amazing sites.

Yet, Billy and Linc preferred the time spent over Central Park. They never tired of exploring the cool green space. Felix appeared to favor the park as well. More often he would head to the park's quiet and peaceful areas.

Felix would fly to Summit Rock and sprawl out in its small grassy meadow with both boys at his side. Together they would study the night sky with all the constellations.

Another favorite place was Bow Bridge, with its graceful curves spanning sixty feet over the lake. The trio would dive under its iron archways low enough to drag their feet in the water below.

Late on these nights Felix might fly directly under the canopy of trees lining the Mall to land on the Bethesda Fountain sculpture. Here they would perch in order to gaze at the lake beyond.

Every summer day was filled with anticipation for the evening's adventures, whether they were rides above the Ramble or dashing over Strawberry Fields. The boys were positive that Central Park was a more magical place than they had ever imagined.

These journeys with Felix had opened their eyes to the possibilities of adventure. They shared a growing desire to know more about the world around them. This yearning sent them to the New York City Public Library for books about the world's great explorers. Armed with stories of great adventurers, Billy and Linc discussed a future searching beyond New York City and imagined what they might encounter.

As summer nights became chilly and autumn was tinting the trees in the park, Felix began to change. The boys noticed that Felix was getting smaller. To their increasing concern soon they could only fit one at a time on his back. Before long he was too small to carry even one boy into the night sky.

Alarmed, they questioned its cause. Billy and Linc knew that Felix relied on the care they supplied. Worried that they were not doing enough, they took extra special care with his food and exercise, but nothing worked. Billy and Linc felt helpless as he continued to shrink. What could be wrong?

By early September it was obvious that Felix was shrinking more and more each day. Nothing the boys did could stop it. Eventually his wings disappeared. It became clear to both boys that Felix resembled more and more the lizard that had hatched in the basement. He was now so small they could cradle him in their hands once again.

Late one night, as they curled together on the floor with Felix between them, Billy and Linc reluctantly acknowledged what was happening. They finally understood that Felix came into their lives to help them grow up. He taught them responsibility, caring and trust. Felix and his nighttime flights fueled their interest in the never-ending wonders of exploration. Most importantly, the shared secret of Felix deepened their friendship. It was a bond for life.

The boys realized it was the time for Felix to go to another child. Billy tenderly embraced Felix. He looked at Linc and they knew what to do.

And so it was on another warm autumn night that Billy and Linc headed to the statue of Hans Christian Andersen by the Conservatory Water. This was the place most loved by Felix for this was a place where children came to hear magical stories.

With tears brimming in their eyes, each boy gave him one last hug. Linc quietly passed Felix to Billy and Billy gently placed him on the ground. Felix looked up at them and smiled one last time. Unable to watch, both boys dropped their heads and closed their eyes before Felix scampered away.

So Remember,

Somewhere out there a
flying dragon waits.
He waits for a child who loves, cares,
dreams, hopes and believes.

Felix waits ...

About the Author

Co-authors and siblings, Karen Furst and James Ainsworth, grew up in the early 50's in suburban New Jersey. It was an era in which television played a smaller role in early development than today. Both of their parents were avid readers and story tellers who encouraged imaginative activities. Felix is based on a series of bedtime stories that their Father created for them so many years ago.

Karen Furst resides in Verona NJ. After many fulfilling years as a grammar school teacher in Harrington Park, NJ, she studied interior design at Parsons in NYC. She co-founded the design firm, Nicholas Ainsworth Ltd in 1983. During those years she worked closely with the illustrator, Ron McCarty, to bring her design concepts to life. Recently retired, Karen is delighted to have the opportunity to work closely with her brother, James, on this project.

James Ainsworth recently retired to Simpsonville, South Carolina. He loves the southern way of life, which he first experienced as a student in Southern Mississippi and Memphis, Tennessee. He fills his leisure time with golf and fishing. James is planning new adventures for Felix and reminds us "Never stop dreaming—that is what keeps you young".

CPSIA information can be obtained
at www.ICGtesting.com
Printed in the USA
LVHW071642280621
691357LV00015B/2100